Leather Shoe Charlie

Written by Gyeong-hwa Kim
Illustrated by Anna & Elena Balbusso
Edited by Joy Cowley

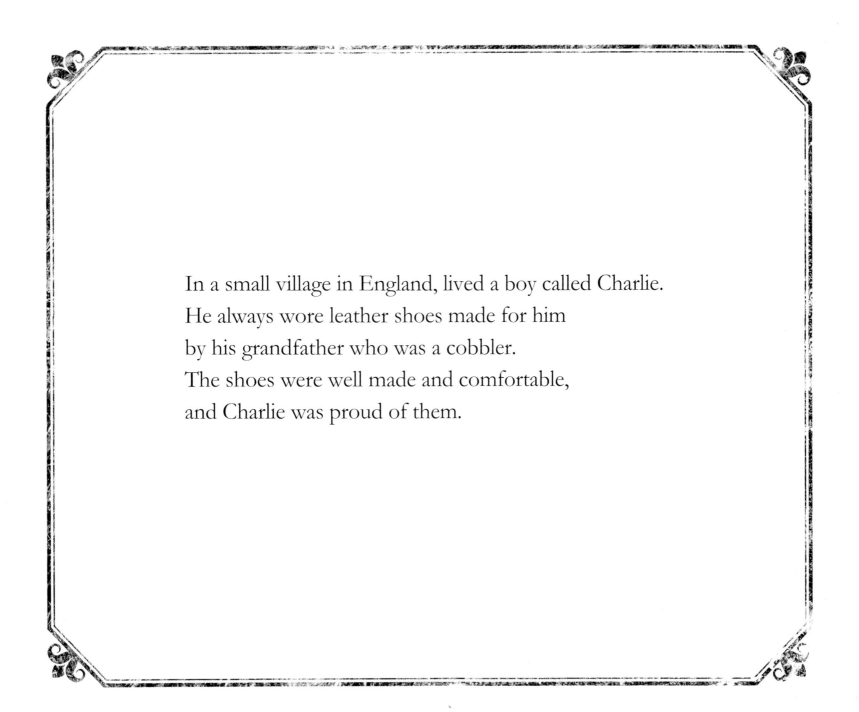

In a small village in England, lived a boy called Charlie.
He always wore leather shoes made for him
by his grandfather who was a cobbler.
The shoes were well made and comfortable,
and Charlie was proud of them.

But people were leaving
the small village.
One family after another went away
until the village was almost empty.
There was no one to buy
Grandfather's shoes,
and by the end of winter,
Charlie's family decided
to move to the city of Manchester*.

*Manchester was at the centre of industrial
development during the Industrial Revolution
and it had many fabric factories.

7

The train station was crowded
with people, all going to the city
to find jobs.
Charlie didn't want to leave home.
His dad said to Grandfather,
"Don't worry. There are many
textile factories. I'm sure I'll get
work there."

The train pulled into the station,
hissing smoke and steam,
and it was time to go.

When they arrived in Manchester, Charlie and his brother Edward could not believe their eyes.

They saw a sea of moving people, and tall buildings everywhere, reaching up to the grey sky.

Industry in England changed drastically in the late 18th century with the invention of new machines. This period is called the Industrial Revolution. Manual work was replaced by machines that mass-produced goods. Farmers left the countryside to search for jobs in the cities.

Charlie's family moved to an area called Angel Meadow*,
but there was no green meadow to welcome them.
Their rooms were in an old and dark tenement building.
It was three storeys high and housed several families.
The sun never shone on that Angel Meadow house.

*Angel Meadow is an area in Manchester where many
poor families lived during the time of the Industrial Revolution.

14

Nobody in the place wore leather shoes like Charlie's,
but Charlie did not care that he was different.
Every step he took on those dark muddy streets
reminded him of his village and his grandfather.
He would look down at his shoes and think,
"One day, I'm going to make shoes too."

Charlie's family worked
in a textile factory where huge
machines clanked all day,
turning out rolls of fabric.
People had to work hard
to keep up with the machines,
and Charlie, along with other
children, had to clean
the machines and carry coal.

Young children worked in textile factories during the Industrial Revolution. When the thread in weaving machines broke, they had to crawl under the machines and tie the ends of the thread together. The space was too small for adults.

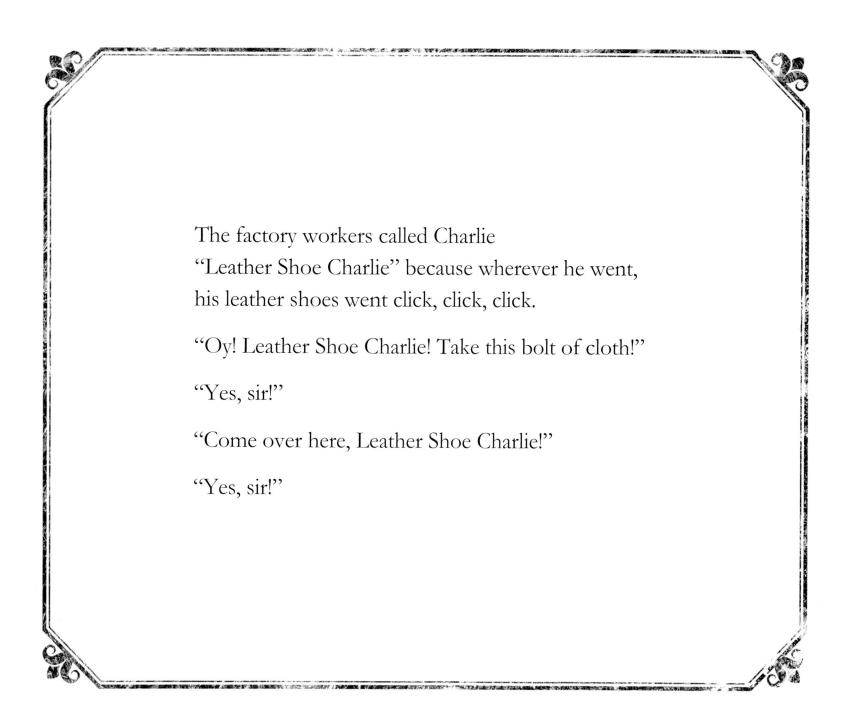

The factory workers called Charlie
"Leather Shoe Charlie" because wherever he went,
his leather shoes went click, click, click.

"Oy! Leather Shoe Charlie! Take this bolt of cloth!"

"Yes, sir!"

"Come over here, Leather Shoe Charlie!"

"Yes, sir!"

Life in Manchester
was different from the village.
Late nights were spent
working at the factory
and the air was always grey
with thick chimney smoke.
Cough, cough! Mum's cough
did not seem to get better,
and Dad looked as though
he was getting smaller.

Cough, cough, cough!
The bad conditions at the factory
made Mum's cough worse.
No one got the rest they needed,
but they didn't dare say anything.
If anyone complained to the boss
they could lose their job.
There were plenty of people
waiting outside the factory
for a chance to work.

Charlie heard Mum and some women
talking. "Tea is good for a cough."

"Who can afford to buy tea
on the money we make?" said Mum.

On Saturday evening, Charlie
and his mother went to the night
market near the factory.
The market sold all sorts of things
such as flour, potatoes, salt and oats.
While Mum bought groceries,
Charlie looked for some tea.
But it was very expensive
and he didn't have enough money.

That night, Mum coughed for hours.
Charlie slipped out of bed
and went back to the market.
"Sir, I'd like to exchange these shoes
for some tea. They're good shoes,
made of leather by my grandfather."

The man said, "Do you really want
to exchange them for some tea?"

Charlie nodded.

The shop owner took the shoes
and handed Charlie a bag of tea.

Charlie woke early, got out of bed,
and boiled some water in the kettle.
He made a cup of hot tea
and gave it to his mother.

"Charlie, where did you get this?"
she asked him.

He didn't answer. He looked at his feet.

Even without his shoes,
he thought of himself
as Leather Shoe Charlie.

One day he would make shoes
just like his grandfather,
and walk again, *click, click, click,*
in beautiful leather shoes.

The Start of the Industrial Revolution

Hello, boys and girls,

I am Charlie from Manchester, United Kingdom.
Did you enjoy my story about Angel Meadow?
The Industrial Revolution brought great changes.
Smoky factories were built in the cities
and massive machines took over the tasks
that were traditionally done by hand.
But the increased supply of goods
did not improve our standard of living.
In the city we could not grow our own food
and the rents were so high that even children
had to go out to work in the factories.
Although I work in a factory at the moment,
I dream of becoming a cobbler
like my grandfather in the village.
I am sure that my dream will come true.

Sincerely,

Charlie

et's Think

When did industrialisation first begin?

How has industry changed the world?

What remains the same today
in spite of industrialisation?

UNITED KINGDOM: Charlie's Homeland

Area: 244,101 km²
Capital: London
Major Language: English

The United Kingdom of Great Britain consists of islands located in the north-west of the European continent. These islands contain England, Scotland, Wales and Northern Ireland. The United Kingdom still has a queen and a royal family.

Coal and the Steam Engine Coal powered industrialisation in the United Kingdom. The demand for coal increased when burning firewood was banned. Because coal reaches higher temperatures than wood, it was used in steam engines which worked using steaming hot water. Steam engines were invented to haul coal out of the ground. This technology led to further inventions including factory looms, and locomotives that pulled trains. The steam engine played a crucial role in the Industrial Revolution.

The Economy of the United Kingdom The United Kingdom was the first country to undergo industrialisation. Factories were built in every city to produce goods. Because of this, the United Kingdom was once called "a factory of the world". The principle exports of the United Kingdom today are the financial, shipping and service industries.

The Industrial Revolution The Industrial Revolution refers to the period in the mid-18th century in which major technological innovations led to great social and economic changes. Countless factories were built. Machines produced cotton fabrics. As machines produced more and more goods, more coal was required to fuel the machines. Train tracks were laid so that trains could transport coal to cities. Since coal is not a clean-burning fuel, smog filled the air and the cities seldom saw blue skies.

Steam locomotive

33

Industrialisation and the Cities

Cities during the Industrial Revolution were heavily populated with people who worked in factories. As people migrated into cities for employment, housing and food supplies became scarce. The thick smog from factory emissions, contributed to the ill health of the people who lived and worked in poor conditions.

A weaving factory during the Industrial Revolution

The Consequences of Industrialisation

Factories were built on farmland, changing rural communities into urban communities, and people living in the country migrated to cities. Machines replaced humans in production lines, and city dwellers consumed the goods produced. The number of artisans and craftsmen dwindled as machines mass-produced goods. Routes were rapidly developed to transport merchandise and coal – roads, railway tracks and canals. This led to increased business exchange between cities. People could relocate easily.

The Life of the Factory Worker

Rapid industrialisation brought wealth to factory owners but poverty to factory workers. Their health deteriorated due to poor working and living conditions, and inferior water systems meant that people could not drink from household taps. Young children did not attend school but instead worked in factories. Many children died from diseases and workplace accidents.

An Unchanging Factor

Industrialisation changed civilization forever, but one factor remains unchanged: people's love and consideration for each other. Relationships between family members, colleagues and neighbours remain true. Mutual respect has become especially important today with increasing work hours and the construction of large residential complexes. We live in a society where what affects one person, affects another. As long as people have healthy attitudes towards each other, we will all remain rich at heart.

Poverty in the city

Let's Talk

Ways to peacefully co-exist in the city:

1. Be considerate of your neighbours: do not run or make loud noises.

2. Greet your neighbours and give them a pleasant smile.

3. Always be mindful of one another.